First Love

And Other Fascinating Stories Of Spanish Life

By

Emilia Pardo-Bazan And Others

Double 9 BOOKS

First Love

And Other Fascinating Stories Of Spanish Life

by Emilia Pardo-Bazan And Others

ISBN: 978-93-61428-32-6

Published by

DOUBLE 9 BOOKS
2/13-B, Ansari Road
Daryaganj, New Delhi – 110002
info@double9books.com
www.double9books.com
Tel. 011-40042856

ABOUT THE AUTHOR

Emilia Pardo-Bazan, a well-known Spanish author and pioneer of feminist literature, is a significant character in the Spanish literary heritage. Her masterpiece, "First Love and Other Fascinating Stories of Spanish Life," demonstrates her extraordinary knack for creating compelling narratives that dive into the complexities of Spanish life. Pardo-Bazan's collection of intriguing stories delves into the depths of human emotions, relationships, and society standards. "First Love" is a moving portrayal of the sweet yet tumultuous nature of love, and the accompanying stories provide valuable insights into various parts of Spanish life. Pardo-Bazan's storytelling prowess is evident in her ability to create rich plots, vivid settings, and profoundly nuanced characters. From stories of forbidden love to investigations into social class and gender dynamics, each story provides an engrossing view into the varied tapestry of Spanish society. As a female icon and literary star, Pardo-Bazan's works continue to connect with readers all over the world, transcending time and culture. "First Love and Other Fascinating Stories of Spanish Life" is a monument to her ongoing legacy, enabling readers to immerse themselves in the rich tapestry of Spanish life and culture woven by one of the country's most celebrated literary voices.

CONTENTS

FIRST LOVE

Emilia Pardo-Bazan

How old was I then? Eleven or twelve years? More probably thirteen, for before then is too early to be seriously in love; but I won't venture to be certain, considering that in Southern countries the heart matures early, if that organ is to blame for such perturbations.

If I do not remember well *when*, I can at least say exactly *how* my first love revealed itself. I was very fond—as soon as my aunt had gone to church to perform her evening devotions—of slipping into her bedroom and rummaging her chest of drawers, which she kept in admirable order. Those drawers were to me a museum; in them I always came across something rare or antique, which exhaled an archaic and mysterious scent, the aroma of the sandalwood fans which perfumed her white linen. Pin-cushions of satin now faded; knitted mittens, carefully wrapped in tissue paper; prints of saints; sewing materials; a reticule of blue velvet embroidered with bugles, an amber and silver rosary would appear from the corners: I used to ponder over them, and return them to their place. But one day—I remember as well as if it were today—in the corner of the top drawer, and lying on some collars of old lace, I saw something gold glittering—I put in my hand, unwittingly crumpled the lace, and drew out a portrait, an ivory miniature, about three inches long, in a frame of gold.

I was struck at first sight. A sunbeam streamed through the window and fell upon the alluring form, which seemed to wish to step out of its dark background and come towards me. It was the most lovely creature, such as I had never seen except in the dreams of my adolescence. The lady of the portrait must have been some twenty odd years; she was no simple maiden, no half-opened rosebud, but a woman in the full resplendency of her beauty. Her face was oval, but not too long, her lips full, half-open and smiling, her eyes cast a languishing side-glance, and she had a dimple on her chin as if formed by the tip of Cupid's playful finger. Her head-dress was strange but elegant; a compact group of curls plastered conewise one over the other covered her temples, and a basket of braided hair rose on the top of her head. This old-fashioned head-dress, which was trussed up from the nape of her neck, disclosed all the softness of her fresh young throat, on which the dimple of her chin was reduplicated more vaguely and delicately.

As for the dress—I do not venture to consider whether our grandmothers were less modest than our wives are, or if the confessors of past times were more indulgent than those of the present; I am inclined to think the latter, for seventy years ago women prided themselves upon being Christianlike and devout, and would not have disobeyed the director of their conscience in so grave and important a matter. What is undeniable is, that if in the present day any lady were to present herself in the garb of the lady of the portrait, there would be a scandal; for from her waist (which began at her armpits) upwards, she was only veiled by light folds of diaphanous gauze, which marked out, rather than covered, two mountains of snow, between which meandered a thread of pearls. With further lack of modesty she stretched out two rounded arms worthy of Juno, ending in finely molded hands—when I say *hands* I am not exact, for, strictly speaking, only one hand could be seen, and that held a richly embroidered handkerchief.

Even today I am astonished at the startling effect which the contemplation of that miniature produced upon me, and how I remained in ecstasy, scarcely breathing, devouring the portrait with my eyes. I had already seen here and there prints representing beautiful women. It often happened that in the illustrated papers, in the mythological engravings of our dining-room, or in a shop-window, that a beautiful face, or a harmonious and graceful figure attracted my precociously artistic gaze. But the miniature encountered in my aunt's drawer, apart from its great beauty, appeared to me as if animated by a subtle and vital breath; you could see it was not the caprice of a painter, but the image of a real and actual person of flesh and blood. The warm and rich tone of the tints made you surmise that the blood was tepid beneath that mother-of-pearl skin. The lips were slightly parted to disclose the enameled teeth; and to complete the illusion there ran round the frame a border of natural hair, chestnut in color, wavy and silky, which had grown on the temples of the original.

As I have said, it was more than a copy, it was the reflection of a living person from whom I was only separated by a wall of glass.—I seized it, breathed upon it, and it seemed to me that the warmth of the mysterious deity communicated itself to my lips and circulated through my veins. At this moment I heard footsteps in the corridor. It was my aunt returning from her prayers. I heard her asthmatic cough, and the dragging of her gouty feet. I had only just time to put the miniature into the drawer, shut it, and approach the window, adopting an innocent and indifferent attitude.

My aunt entered noisily, for the cold of the church had exasperated her catarrh, now chronic. Upon seeing me, her wrinkled eyes brightened, and giving me a friendly tap with her withered hand, she asked me if I had been turning over her drawers as usual.

Then, with a chuckle:

"Wait a bit, wait a bit," she added, "I have something for you, something you will like."

And she pulled out of her vast pocket a paper bag, and out of the bag three or four gum lozenges, sticking together in a cake, which gave me a feeling of nausea.

My aunt's appearance did not invite one to open one's mouth and devour these sweets: the course of years, her loss of teeth, her eyes dimmed to an unusual degree, the sprouting of a mustache or bristles on her sunken-in mouth, which was three inches wide, dull gray locks fluttering above her sallow temples, a neck flaccid and livid as the crest of the turkey when in a good temper.—In short, I did not take the lozenges. Ugh! A feeling of indignation, a manly protest rose in me, and I said forcibly:

"I do not want it, I don't want it."

"You don't want it? What a wonder! You who are greedier than a cat!"

"I am not a little boy," I exclaimed, drawing myself up, and standing on tiptoes; "I don't care for sweets."

My aunt looked at me half good-humoredly and half ironically, and at last, giving way to the feeling of amusement I caused her, burst out laughing, by which she disfigured herself, and exposed the horrible anatomy of her jaws. She laughed so heartily that her chin and nose met, hiding her lips, and emphasizing two wrinkles, or rather two deep furrows, and more than a dozen lines on her cheeks and eyelids; at the same time her head and body shook with the laughter, until at last her cough began to interrupt the bursts, and between laughing and coughing the old lady involuntarily spluttered all over my face. Humiliated, and full of disgust, I escaped rapidly thence to my mother's room, where I washed myself with soap and water, and began to muse on the lady of the portrait.

And from that day and hour I could not keep my thoughts from her. As soon as my aunt went out, to slip into her room, open the drawer, bring out the miniature, and lose myself in contemplation, was the work of a minute. By dint of looking at it, I fancied that her languishing eyes, through the voluptuous veiling, of her eyelashes, were fixed in mine, and that her white bosom heaved. I became ashamed to kiss her, imagining she would be annoyed at my audacity, and only pressed her to my heart or held her against my cheek. All my actions and thoughts referred to the lady; I behaved towards her with the most extraordinary refinement and super-delicacy. Before entering my aunt's room and opening the longed-for drawer, I washed, combed my hair, and tidied myself, as I have seen since is usually done before repairing to a love appointment.

I often happened to meet in the street other boys of my age, very proud of their slip of a sweetheart, who would exultingly show me love-letters, photographs, and flowers, and who asked me if I hadn't a sweetheart with whom to correspond. A feeling of inexplicable bashfulness tied my tongue, and I only replied with an enigmatic and haughty smile. And when they questioned me as to what I thought of the beauty of their little maidens, I would shrug my shoulders and disdainfully call them *ugly mugs*.

One Sunday I went to play in the house of some little girl-cousins, really very pretty, the eldest of whom was not yet fifteen. We were amusing ourselves looking into a stereoscope, when suddenly one of the little girls, the youngest, who counted twelve summers at most, secretly seized my hand, and in some confusion and blushing as red as a brazier, whispered in my ear:

"Take this."

At the same time I felt in the palm of my hand something soft and fresh, and saw that it was a rosebud with its green foliage. The little girl ran away smiling and casting a side-glance at me; but I, with a Puritanism worthy of Joseph, cried out in my turn:

"Take this!"

And I threw the rosebud at her nose, a rebuff which made her tearful and pettish with me the whole afternoon, and for which she has not pardoned me even now, though she is married and has three children.

The two or three hours which my aunt spent morning and evening together at church being too short for my admiration of the entrancing portrait, I resolved at last to keep the miniature in my pocket, and went about all day hiding myself from people just as if I had committed some crime. I fancied that the portrait from the depth of its prison of cloth could see all my actions, and I arrived at such a ridiculous extremity, that if I wanted to scratch myself, pull up my sock, or do anything else not in keeping with the idealism of my chaste love, I first drew out the miniature, put it in a safe place, and then considered myself free to do whatever I wanted. In fact, since I had accomplished the theft, there was no limit to my vagaries. At night I hid it under the pillow, and slept in an attitude of defense; the portrait remained near the wall, I outside, and I awoke a thousand times, fearing somebody would come to bereave me of my treasure. At last I drew it from beneath the pillow and slipped it between my nightshirt and left breast, on which the following day could be seen the imprint of the chasing of the frame.

The contact of the dear miniature gave me delicious dreams. The lady of the portrait, not in effigy, but in her natural size and proportions, alive, graceful, affable, beautiful, would come towards me to conduct me to her palace by a rapid and flying train. With sweet authority she would make me sit on a stool at her feet, and would pass her beautifully molded hand over my head, caressing my brow, my eyes, and loose curls. I read to her out of a big missal, or played the lute, and she deigned to smile, thanking me for the pleasure which my reading and songs gave her. At last romantic reminiscences overflowed in my brain, and sometimes I was a page, and sometimes a troubadour.

With all these fanciful ideas, the fact is that I began to grow thin quite perceptibly, which was observed with great disquietude in my parents and my aunt.

"In this dangerous and critical age of development, everything is alarming," said my father, who used to read books of medicine, and anxiously studied my dark eyelids, my dull eyes, my contracted and pale lips, and above all, the complete lack of appetite which had taken possession of me.

"Play, boy; eat, boy," he would say to me, and I replied to him, dejectedly:

"I don't feel inclined."

They began to talk of distractions, offered to take me to the theater; stopped my studies, and gave me foaming new milk to drink. Afterwards they poured cold water over my head and back to fortify my nerves; and I noticed that my father at table or in the morning when I went to his bedroom to bid him good morning, would gaze at me fixedly for some little time, and would sometimes pass his hand down my spine, feeling the vertebrae. I hypocritically lowered my eyes, resolved to die rather than confess my crime. As soon as I was free from the affectionate solicitude of my family, I found myself alone with my lady of the portrait. At last, to get nearer to her, I thought I would do away with the cold crystal. I trembled upon putting this into execution; but at last my love prevailed over the vague fear with which such a profanation filled me, and with skillful cunning I succeeded in pulling away the glass and exposing the ivory plate. As I pressed my lips to the painting I could scent the slight fragrance of the border of hair, I imagined to myself even more realistically that it was a living person whom I was grasping with my trembling hands. A feeling of faintness overpowered me, and I fell unconscious on the sofa, tightly holding the miniature.

When I came to my senses I saw my father, my mother, and my aunt, all bending anxiously over me; I read their terror and alarm in their faces; my father was feeling my pulse, shaking his head, and murmuring:

"His pulse is nothing but a flutter, you can scarcely feel it."

My aunt, with her claw-like fingers, was trying to take the portrait from me, and I was mechanically hiding it and grasping it more firmly.

"But, my dear boy—let go, you are spoiling it!" she exclaimed. "Don't you see you are smudging it? I am not scolding you, my dear.—I will show it to you as often as you like, but don't destroy it; let go, you are injuring it."

"Let him have it," begged my mother, "the boy is not well."

"Of all things to ask!" replied the old maid. "Let him have it! And who will paint another like this—or make me as I was then? Today nobody paints miniatures—it is a thing of the past, and I also am a thing of the past, and I am not what is represented there!"

My eyes dilated with horror; my fingers released their hold on the picture. I don't know how I was able to articulate:

"You—the portrait—is you?"

"Don't you think I am as pretty now, boy? Bah! one is better looking at twenty-three than at—than at—I don't know what, for I have forgotten how old I am!"

My head drooped and I almost fainted again; anyway, my father lifted me in his arms on to the bed, and made me swallow some tablespoonfuls of port.

I recovered very quickly, and never wished to enter my aunt's room again.

AN ANDALUSIAN DUEL

Serafin Estebanez Calderon

Through the little square of St. Anna, towards a certain tavern, where the best wine is to be quaffed in Seville, there walked in measured steps two men whose demeanor clearly manifested the soil which gave them birth. He who walked in the middle of the street, taller than the other by about a finger's length, sported with affected carelessness the wide, slouched hat of Ecija, with tassels of glass beads and a ribbon as black as his sins. He wore his cloak gathered under his left arm; the right, emerging from a turquoise lining, exposed the merino lambskin with silver clasps. The herdsman's boots—white, with Turkish buttons,—the breeches gleaming red from below the cloak and covering the knee, and, above all, his strong and robust appearance, dark curly hair, and eye like a red-hot coal, proclaimed at a distance that all this combination belonged to one of those men who put an end to horses between their knees and tire out the bull with their lance.

He walked on, arguing with his companion, who was rather spare than prodigal in his person, but marvelously lithe and supple. The latter was shod with low shoes, garters united the stockings to the light-blue breeches, the waistcoat was cane-colored, his sash light green, and jaunty shoulder-knots, lappets, and rows of buttons ornamented the carmelite jacket. The open cloak, the hat drawn over his ear, his short, clean steps, and the manifestations in all his limbs and movements of agility and elasticity beyond trial plainly showed that in the arena, carmine cloth in hand, he would mock at the most frenzied of Jarama bulls, or the best horned beasts from Utrera.

I—who adore and die for such people, though the compliment be not returned—went slowly in the wake of their worships, and, unable to restrain myself, entered with them the same tavern, or rather eating-house, since there they serve certain provocatives as well as wine, and I, as my readers perceive, love to call things by their right name. I entered and sat down at once, and in such a manner as not to interrupt Oliver and Roland, and that they might not notice me, when I saw that, as if believing themselves alone, they threw their arms with an amicable gesture round each others' neck, and thus began their discourse:

"Pulpete," said the taller, "now that we are going to meet each other, knife in hand—you here, I there,—*one, two,—on your guard,—triz, traz,—have that,—take this and call it what you like*—let us first drain a tankard to the music and measure of some songs."

"Señor Balbeja," replied Pulpete, drawing his face aside and spitting with the greatest neatness and pulchritude towards his shoe, "I am not the kind of man either for La Gorja or other similar earthly matters, or because a steel tongue is sheathed in my body, or my weasand slit, or for any other such trifle, to be provoked or vexed with such a friend as Balbeja. Let the wine be brought, and then, we will sing; and afterwards blood—blood to the hilt."

The order was given, they clinked glasses, and, looking one at the other, sang a Sevillian song.

This done, they threw off their cloaks with an easy grace, and unsheathed their knives with which to prick one another, the one Flemish with a white haft, the other from Guadix, with a guard to the hilt, both blades dazzling in their brightness, and sharpened and ground enough for operating upon cataracts, much less ripping up bellies and bowels. The two had already cleft the air several times with the said lancets, their cloak wound round their left arm—first drawing closer, then back, now more boldly and in bounds—when Pulpete hoisted the flag for parley, and said:

"Balbeja, my friend, I only beg you to do me the favor not to fan my face with *Juilon* your knife, since a slash might use it so ill that my mother who bore me would not know me, and I should not like to be considered ugly; neither is it right to mar and destroy what God made in His likeness."

"Agreed," replied Balbeja; "I will aim lower."

"Except—except my stomach also, for I was ever a friend to cleanliness, and I should not like to see myself fouled in a bad way, if your knife and arm played havoc with my liver and intestines."

"I will strike higher; but let us go on."

"Take care of my chest, it was always weak."

"Then just tell me, friend, *where* am I to sound or tap you?"

"My dear Balbeja, there's always plenty of time and space to hack at a man; I have here on my left arm a wen, of which you can make meat as much as you like."

"Here goes for it," said Balbeja, and he hurled himself like an arrow; the other warded off the thrust with his cloak, and both, like skilful penmen, began again tracing S's and signatures in the air with dashes and flourishes without, however, raising a particle of skin.

I do not know what would have been the end of this onslaught, since my venerable, dry, and shriveled person was not suitable for forming a point of exclamation between two combatants; and the tavern-keeper troubled so little about what was happening that he drowned the stamping of their feet and clatter of the tumbling stools and utensils by scraping street music on a guitar as loud as he could. Otherwise he was as calm as if he were entertaining two angels instead of two devils incarnate.

I do not know, I repeat, how this scene would have ended, when there crossed the threshold a parsonage who came to take a part in the development of the drama. There entered, I say, a woman of twenty to twenty-two years of age, diminutive in body, superlative in audacity and grace. Neat and clean hose and shoes, short, black flounced petticoat, a linked girdle, head-dress or mantilla of fringed taffeta caught together at the nape of her neck, and a corner of it over her shoulder, she passed before my eyes with swaying hips, arms akimbo, and moving her head to and fro as she looked about her on all sides.

Upon seeing her the tavern-keeper dropped his instrument, and I was overtaken by perturbation such as I had not experienced for thirty years (I am, after all, only flesh and blood); but, without halting for such lay-figures, she advanced to the field of battle.

There was a lively to-do here; Don Pulpete and Don Balbeja when they saw Doña Gorja appear, first cause of the disturbance and future prize for the victor, increased their feints, flourishes, curvets, onsets, crouching, and bounds—all, however, without touching a hair. Our Helen witnessed in silence for a long time this scene in history with that feminine pleasure which the daughters of Eve enjoy at such critical moments. But gradually her pretty brow clouded over, until, drawing from her delicate ear, not a flower or earring, but the stump of a cigar, she hurled it amidst the jousters. Not even Charles V's cane in the last duel in Spain produced such favorable effects. Both came forward immediately with formal respect, and each, by reason of the discomposure of his person and clothes, presumed to urge a title by which to recommend himself to the fair with the flounces. She, as though pensive, was going over the passage of arms in her mind, and then, with firm and confident resolution, spoke thus:

"And is this affair for me?"

"Who else should it be for? since I—since nobody—" they replied in the same breath.

"Listen, gentlemen," said she. "For females such as I and my parts of my charms and descent—daughter of La Gatusa, niece of La Mêndez and granddaughter of La Astrosa—know that there are neither pacts nor compacts, nor any such futile things, nor are any of them worth a farthing. And when men challenge each other, let the knife do its work and the red blood flow, so as not to have my mother's daughter present without giving her the pleasure of snapping her fingers in the face of the other. If you pretend you are fighting for me, it's a lie; you are wholly mistaken, and that not by halves. I love neither of you. Mingalarios of Zafra is to my taste, and he and I look upon you with scorn and contempt. Good-by, my braves; and, if you like, call my man to account."

She spoke, spat, smoothed the saliva with the point of her shoe, looking Pulpete and Balbeja full in the face, and went out with the same expressive movements with which she entered.

The two unvarnished braggarts followed the valorous Doña Gorja with their eyes; and then with a despicable gesture drew their knives across their sleeve as though wiping off the blood there might have been, sheathed them at one and the same time, and said together:

"Through woman the world was lost, through a woman Spain was lost; but it has never been known, nor do ballads relate, nor the blind beggars sing, nor is it heard in the square or markets, that two valiant men killed each, other for another lover."

"Give me that fist, Don Pulpete."

"Your hand, Don Balbeja."

They spoke and strode out into the street, the best friends in the world, leaving me all amazed at such whimsicality.

MARIQUITA THE BALD

Juan Eugenio Hartzenbusch

It is as sorry a matter to use words of whose meaning one is ignorant as it is a blemish for a man of sense to speak of what he knows nothing about. I say this to those of you who may have the present story in your hands, however often you may have happened to have heard *Mariquita the Bald* mentioned, and I swear by my doublet that you shall soon know who Mariquita the Bald was, as well as I know who ate the Christmas turkey, setting aside the surmise that it certainly must have been a mouth.

I desire, therefore, to enlighten your ignorance of this subject, and beg to inform you that the said noted Maria (Mariquita is a diminutive of Maria) was born in the District of Segovia, and in the town of San Garcia, the which town is famed for the beauty of the maidens reared within its walls, who for the most part have such gentle and lovely faces that may I behold such around me at the hour of my death. Maria's father was an honest farmer, by name Juan Lanas, a Christian old man and much beloved, who had inherited no mean estate from his forefathers, though with but little wit in his crown,—a lack which was the cause of much calamity to both the father and the daughter, for in the times to which we have attained, God forgive me if it is not necessary to have more of the knave than of the fool in one's composition.

Now it came to pass that Juan Lanas, for the castigation of his sins, must needs commit himself to a lawsuit with one of his neighbors about a vine stock which was worth about fifty *maravedis*; and Juan was in the right, and the judges gave the verdict in his favor, so that he won his case, excepting that the suit lasted no less than ten years and the costs amounted to nothing less than fifty thousand *maravedis*, not to speak of a disease of the eyes which, after all was over, left him blind. When he found himself with diminished property and without his eyesight, in sorrow and disgust he turned into money such part of his patrimony as sufficed to rid him of the hungry herd of scriveners and lawyers, and took his way to Toledo with his daughter, who was already entering upon her sixteenth year, and had matured into one of the most beautiful, graceful, and lovable damsels to be found throughout all Castile and the kingdoms beyond.

For she was white as the lily and red like the rose, straight and tall of stature, and slender in the waist, with fair, shapely hips; and again her foot and hand were plump and small to a marvel, and she possessed a head of hair which reached to her knees. For I knew the widow Sarmiento who was their housekeeper, and she told me how she could scarcely clasp Mariquita's hair with both hands, and that she could not comb the hair unless Maria stood up and the housekeeper mounted on a footstool, for if Maria sat down the long tresses swept the ground, and therefore became all entangled.

And do not imagine, her beauty and grace being such, that she sinned greatly in pride and levity, as is the wont of girls in this age. She was as humble as a cloistered lay-sister, and as silent as if she were not a woman, and patient as the sucking lamb, and industrious as the ant, clean as the ermine, and pure as a saint of those times in which, by the grace of the Most High, saintly women were born into the world. But I must confide to you in friendship that our Mariquita was not a little vain about her hair, and loved to display it, and for this reason, now in the streets, now when on a visit, now when at mass, it is said she used to subtilely loosen her mantilla so that her tresses streamed down her back, the while feigning forgetfulness and carelessness. She never wore a hood, for she said it annoyed her and choked her; and every time that her father reproached her for some deed deserving of punishment and threatened to cut off her hair, I warrant you she suffered three times more than after a lash from the whip, and would then be good for three weeks successively; so much so that Juan Lanas, perceiving her amendment, would laugh under his cloak, and when saying his say to his gossips would tell them that his daughter, like the other saint of Sicily, would reach heaven by her hair.

Having read so far, you must now know that Juan Lanas, the blind man, with the change of district and dwelling did not change his judgment and if he was crack-brained at San Garcia, he remained crack-brained at Toledo, consuming in this resort his money upon worthless drugs and quacks which did not cure his blindness and impoverished him more and more every day, so that if his daughter had not been so dexterous with her fingers in making and broidering garments of linen, wool, and silk, I promise you that this miserable Juan would have had to go for more than four Sundays without a clean shirt to put on or a mouthful to eat, unless he had begged it from door to door.

The years passed by to find Maria every day more beautiful, and her father every day more blind and more desirous to see, until his affliction and trouble took such forcible possession of his breast and mind, that Maria saw as clear as daylight that if her father did not recover his sight, he would die of grief. Maria thereupon straightway took her father and led him to the house of an Arabian physician of great learning who dwelt at Toledo, and told the Moor to see if there were any cure for the old man's sight. The Arabian examined and touched Juan, and made this and that experiment with him, and everything prospered, in that the physician swore great oaths by the heel-bone of Mohammed that there was a complete certainty of curing Juan and making him to see his daughter again, if only he, the physician, were paid for the cure with five hundred *maravedis* all in gold. A sad termination for such a welcome beginning, for the two unhappy creatures, Juan and Maria, had neither *maravedi* nor *cuarto* in the money box! So they went thence all downcast, and Maria never ceased praying to his Holiness Saint John and his Holiness Saint James (the patron saint of Spain) to repair to their assistance in this sad predicament.

"In what way," conjectured she inwardly, "in what way can I raise five hundred *maravedis* to be quits with the Moor who will give back his sight to my poor old father? All! I have it. I am a pretty maid, and suitors innumerable, commoners and nobles, pay their addresses and compliments to me. But all are trifling youths who only care for love-making and who seek light o' loves rather than spouses according to the law of the Lord Jesus Christ. I remember, notwithstanding, that opposite our house lives the sword-cutler, Master Palomo, who is always looking at me and never speaks to me, and the Virgin assist me, he appears a man of very good condition for a husband; but what maiden, unless she were cross-eyed, or hunch-backed, could like a man with such a flat nose, with that skin the color of a ripe date, with those eyes like a dead calf's, and with those huge hands, which are more like the paws of a wild beast that the belongings of a person who with them should softly caress the woman whom Destiny bestows upon him for a companion? 'Tis said that he is no drunkard, nor cudgeler, nor dallier with women, nor a liar, and that he is besides possessed of much property and very rich. Pity 'tis that one who is so ugly and stiff-necked should unite such parts."

Thus turning the matter over and over in her mind, Maria together with Juan reached their home, where was awaiting them an esquire in a long mourning robe, who told Maria that the aunt of the mayor of the city had died in an honest estate and in the flower of her age, for she had not yet completed her seventy years, and that the obsequies of this sexagenarian damsel were to be performed the following day, on which occasion her coffin would be carried to the church by maidens, and he was come to ask Maria if she would please to be one of the bearers of the dead woman, for which she would receive a white robe, and to eat, and ducat, and thanks into the bargain.

Maria, since she was a well-brought-up maid, replied that if it seemed well to her father, it would also seem well to her.

Juan accepted, and Maria was rejoiced to be able to make a display of her hair, for it is well known that the maidens who bear one another to the grave walk with disheveled locks. And when on the morrow the tiring-women of the mayoress arrayed Maria in a robe white as the driven snow and fine as the skin of an onion; and when they girt her slender waist with a sash of crimson silk, the ends of which hung down to the broad hem of the skirt; and when they crowned her smooth and white forehead with a wreath of white flowers, I warrant you that, what with the robe and the sash and the wreath, and the beautiful streaming hair and her lovely countenance and gracious mien, she seemed no female formed of flesh and blood, but a superhuman creature or blessed resident of those shining circles in which dwell the celestial hierarchies. The mayor and the other mourners stepped forth to see her, and all unceasingly praised God, who was pleased to perform such miracles for the consolation and solace of those living in this world.

And there in a corner of the hall, motionless like a heap of broken stones, stood one of the mutes with the hood of his long cloak covering his head, so that nothing could be seen but his eyes, the which he kept fixed on the fair damsel. The latter modestly lowered her eyes to the ground with her head a little bent and her cheeks red for bashfulness, although it pleased her no little to hear the praises of her beauty. At this moment a screen was pushed aside, and there began to appear a huge bulk of petticoats, which was nothing less than the person of the mayoress, for she was with child and drawing near to her time. And when she saw Maria, she started, opened her eyes a hand's-breadth wide, bit her lips, and called hurriedly for her husband. They stepped aside for a good while, and then hied them thence, and when they returned the mutes and maidens had all gone.

While they were burying the defunct lady I must tell you, curious readers, that the mayor and mayoress had been married for many years without having any children, and they longed for them like the countryman for rain in the month of May, and at last her hour of bliss came to the mayoress, to the great content of her husband. Now, it was whispered that the said lady had always been somewhat capricious; judge for yourselves what she would be now in the time of her pregnancy! And as she was already on the way to fifty, she was more than mediocrely bald and hairless, and on these very same days had commissioned a woman barber, who lived in the odor of witchcraft, to prepare for her some false hair, but it was not to be that of a dead woman, for the mayoress said very sensibly that if the hair belonged to a dead woman who rejoiced in supreme glory, or was suffering for her sins in purgatory, it would be profanation to wear any pledge of theirs, and if they were in hell, it was a terrible thing to wear on one's person relics of one of the damned. And when the mayoress saw the abundant locks of Maria, she coveted them for herself, and it was for this reason that she called to the mayor to speak to her in private and besought him eagerly to persuade Mario to allow herself to be shorn upon the return from the burial.

"I warn you," said the mayor, "that you are desirous of entering upon a very knotty bargain, for the disheveled girl idolizes her hair in such wise that she would sooner lose a finger than suffer one of her tresses to be cut off."

"I warn you," replied the mayoress, "that if on this very day the head of this young girl is not shorn smooth beneath my hand as a melon, the child to which I am about to give birth will have a head of hair on its face, and if it happens to be a female, look you, a pretty daughter is in store for you!"

"But bethink yourself that Maria will ask, who knows, a good few crowns for this shaving."

"Bethink yourself that if not, your heir or heiress, begotten after many years' marriage, will come amiss; and bear in mind, by the way, that we are not so young as to hope to replace this by another."

Upon this she turned her back to the mayor, and went to her apartment crying out: "I want the hair, I must have the hair, and if I do not get the hair, by my halidom I shall never become a mother."

In the meantime the funeral had taken place without any novelty to mention, excepting that if in the streets any loose fellow in the crowd assayed to annoy the fair Maria, the hooded mute, of whom we made mention before, quickly drew from beneath his cloak a strap, with which he gave a lash to the insolent rogue without addressing one word to him, and then walked straight on as if nothing had happened. When all the mourners returned, the mayor seized hold of Maria's hand and said to her:

"And now, fair maid, let us withdraw for a little while into this other apartment," and thus talking whilst in motion he brought her into his wife's private tiring-room, and sat himself down in a chair and bent his head and stroked his beard with the mien of one who is studying what beginning to give his speech. Maria, a little foolish and confused, remained standing in front of the mayor, and she also humbly lowered before him her eyes, black as the sloe; and to occupy herself with something, gently fingered the ends of the sash, which girded her waist and hung down over her skirt, not knowing what to expect from the grave mien and long silence of the mayor, who, raising his eyes and looking up at Maria, when he beheld her in so modest a posture, devised thence a motive with which to begin, saying:

"Forsooth, Maria, so modest and sanctimonious is thy bearing, that it is easy to see thou art preparing thyself to become a black-wimpled nun. And if it be so, as I presume it to be, I now offer of my own accord to dispose of thy entry into the cloisters without any dowry, on the condition that thou dost give me something that thou hast on thy head, and which then will not be necessary for thee."

"Nay, beshrew me, Sir Mayor," replied Maria, "for I durst not think that the Lord calls upon me to take that step, for then my poor father would remain in the world without the staff of his old age."

"Then, now, I desire to give thee some wise counsel, maid Maria. Thou dost gain thy bread with great fatigue. Thou shouldst make use of thy time as much as is possible. Now one of thy neighbors hath told me that in the dressing of thy hair thou dost waste every day more than an hour. It would be better far if thou didst spend this hour on thy work rather than in the dressing and braiding which thou dost to thy hair."

"That is true, Sir Mayor," replied Maria, turning as red as a carnation, "but, look you, it is not my fault if I have a wealth of tresses, the combing and plaiting of which necessitate so long a time every morning."

"I tell thee it is thy fault," retorted the mayor, "for if thou didst cut off this mane, thou wouldst save thyself all this combing and plaiting, and thus wouldst have more time for work, and so gain more money, and wouldst also give no occasion to people to call thee vain. They even say that the devil will some day carry thee off by thy hair. Nay, do not be distressed, for I already perceive the tears gathering in thine eyes, for thou hast them indeed very ready at hand; I admonish thee for thine own good without any self-interest. Cut thy hair off, shear thyself, shave thyself, good Maria, and to allay the bitterness of the shearing, I will give fifty *maravedis*, always on condition that thou dost hand me over the hair."

When Maria at first heard this offer of so reasonable a sum for this her hair, it seemed to her a jest of the mayor's, and she smiled right sweetly while she dried her tears, repeating:

"You will give me fifty *maravedis* if I shave myself?"

Now it appeared to the mayor (who, it is said, was not gifted with all the prudence of Ulysses) that the smile signified that the maid was not satisfied with so small a price, and he added:

"If thou wilt not be content with fifty *maravedis*, I will give thee a hundred."

Then Maria saw some hangings of the apartment moving in front of her, and perceiving a bulky protuberance, she immediately divined that the mayoress was hiding behind there, and that the protuberance was caused by her portly form. Now she discovered the mayor's design, and that it was probably a caprice of his spouse, and she made a vow not to suffer herself to be shorn unless she acquired by these means the five hundred *maravedis* needful to pay the Arabian physician who would give her father back his eyesight.

Then the mayor raised his price from a hundred *maravedis* to a hundred and fifty, and afterwards to two hundred, and Maria continued her sweet smiling, shaking of the head, and gestures, and every time that the mayor bid higher and Maria feigned to be reluctant, she almost hoped that the mayor would withdraw from his proposition, for the great grief it caused her to despoil herself of that precious ornament, notwithstanding that my means of it she might gain her father's health. Finally the mayor, anxious to conclude the treaty, for he saw the stirring of the curtains, and knew by them the anxiety and state of mind of the listener, closed by saying:

"Go to, hussy, I will give thee five hundred *maravedis*. See, once and for all, if thou canst agree on these terms."

"Be it so," replied Maria, sighing as if her soul would flee from her flesh with these words—"be it so, so long that nobody doth know that I remain bald."

"I will give my word for it," said the mayoress, stepping from behind the curtains with a pair of sharp shears in her hands and a wrapper over her arm.

When Maria saw the scissors she turned as yellow as wax, and when they told her to sit down on the sacrificial chair, she felt herself grow faint and had to ask for a drink of water; and when they tied the wrapper round her throat it is related that she would have immediately torn it asunder if her courage had not failed her. And when at the first movement of the shears she felt the cold iron against her skull, I tell you it seemed to her as if they were piercing her heart with a bright dagger. It is possible that she did not keep her head still for a moment while this tonsuring was taking place; she moved it in spite of herself, now to one side, now to another, to flee from the clipping scissors, of which the rude cuts and the creaking axis wounded her ears. Her posture and movements, however, were of no avail to the poor shorn maiden, and the pertinacious shearer, with the anxiety and covetousness of a pregnant woman satisfying a caprice, seized the hair well, or ill, by handfuls, and went on bravely clipping, and the locks fell on to the white wrapper, slipping down thence till they reached the ground.

At last the business came to an end, and the mayoress, who was beside herself with joy, caressingly passed the palm of her hand again and again over the maid's bald head from the front to the back, saying:

"By my mother's soul, I have shorn you so regularly and close to the root that the most skilful barber could not have shorn you better. Get up and braid the hair while my husband goes to get the money and I your clothes, so that you can leave the house without anyone perceiving it."

The mayor and mayoress went out of the room, and Maria, as soon as she found herself alone, went to look at herself in a mirror that hung there; and when she saw herself bald she lost the patience she had had until then, and groaned with rage and struck herself, and even tried to wrench off her ears, which appeared to her now outrageously large, although they were not so in reality. She stamped upon her hair and cursed herself for having ever consented to lose it, without remembering her father, and just as if she had no father at all. But as it is a quality of human nature to accept what cannot be altered, poor angry Maria calmed down little by little, and she picked up the hair from the ground and bound it together and braided it into great ropes, not without kissing it and lamenting over it many times.

The mayor and the mayoress returned, he with the money and she with the every-day clothes of Maria, who undressed and folded her white robe in a kerchief, put on her old gown, hid herself with her shawl to the eyes, and walked, moaning, to the house of the Moor, without noticing that the man with the hood over his head was following behind her, and that when she, in a moment of forgetfulness, lowered her shawl through the habit she had of displaying her tresses, her bald head could be plainly seen. The Moor received the five hundred *maravedis* with that good-will with which money is always received, and told Maria to bring Juan Lanas to his house to stay there so long as there was any risk in the cure. Maria went to fetch the old man, and kept silence as to her shorn head so as not to grieve him, and whilst Juan remained the physician's guest, Maria durst not leave her home except after nightfall, and then well enveloped. This, however, did not hinder her being followed by the muffled-up man.

One evening the Moor told her in secret that the next morning he would remove the bandages from Juan's eyes. Maria went to bed that night with great rejoicing, but thought to herself that when her father saw her (which would be with no little pleasure) he would be pleased three or four times more if he could see her with the pretty head-dress which she used to wear in her native town. Amidst such cavillation she donned the next day her best petticoat and ribbons to his to the Arabian's house; and while she was sitting down to shoe herself she of a sudden felt something like a hood closing over her head, and, turning round, she saw behind her the muffled-up man of before, who, throwing aside his cloak, discovered himself to be the sword-cutler, Master Palomo, who, without speaking, presented Maria with a little Venetian mirror, in which she looked and saw herself with her own hair and garb in such wise that she wondered for a good time if it were not a dream that the mayoress had shorn her.

The fact was that Master Palomo was a great crony of the old woman barber, and had seen in her house Maria's tresses on the very same afternoon of the morning in which he saw Maria was bald, and keeping silence upon the matter, had wheedled the old woman into keeping Maria's hair for him, and dressing for the mayoress some other hair of the same hue which the crone had from a dead woman—a bargain by which the crafty old dame acquired many a bright crown. And the story relates that as soon as Maria regained her much lamented and sighed-for hair by the hands of the gallant sword-cutler, the master appeared to her much less ugly than before. I do not know if it tells that from that moment she began to look on him with more favorable eyes, but i' sooth it is a fact that upon his asking her to accept his escort to the Moor's house, she gave her assent, and the two set out hand in hand, the maiden holding her head up free from mufflers. As they both entered the physician's apartment her father threw himself into Maria's arms, crying:

"Glory to God, I see thee now, my beloved daughter. How tall and beautiful thou art grown! Verily, it is worth while to become blind for five years to see one's daughter matured thus! Now that I see daylight again, it is only right that I should no longer be a burden to thee. I shall work for myself, for as for thee it is already time for thee to marry."

"For this very purpose am I come," broke in at this opportune moment the silent sword-cutler; "I, as you will have already recognized by my voice, am your neighbor, Master Palomo. I love Maria, and ask you for her hand."

"Lack-a-day, master, but your exterior is not very prepossessing. Howbeit, if Maria doth accept you, I am content."

"I," replied Maria, wholly abashed, and smoothing the false hair (which then weighed upon her head and heart like a burden of five hundred weight)—"I, so may God enlighten me, for I durst not venture to reply."

Palomo took her right hand without saying anything, and as he did so Maria looked at the master's wrists, and observed the wristbands of his shirt, neatly embroidered, and with some suspicion and beating of her heart said to him:

"If you wish to please me, good neighbor, tell me by what seamstress is this work?"

"It is the work," replied the master, jocularly, "the work of a pretty maiden who for five years has toiled for my person, albeit she hath not known it till now."

"Now I perceive," said Maria, "how that all the women who have come to give me linen to sew and embroider were sent by you, and that is why they paid me more than is customary."

The master did not reply, but he smiled and held out his arms to Maria. Maria threw herself into them, embracing him very caressingly; and Juan himself said to the two:

"In good sooth, you are made one for the other."

"By my troth, my beloved one," continued the sword-cutler after a while, "if my countenance had only been more pleasing, I should not have been silent towards you for so many long days, nor would I have been content with, gazing at you from afar. I should have spoken to you, you would have made me the confidant of your troubles, and I would have given you the five hundred *maravedis* for the cure of your good father."

And whispering softly into her ear, he added: "And then you would not have passed that evil moment under the hands of the mayoress. But if you fear that she may break the promise she made to you to keep silence as to your cropped head, let us, if it please you, set out for Seville, where nobody knows you, and thus—"

"No more," exclaimed Maria, resolutely throwing on the ground the hair, which Juan picked up all astonished. "Send this hair to the mayoress, since it was for this and not for that of the dead woman that she paid so dearly. For I, to cure myself of my vanity, now make a vow, with your good permission, to go shorn all my life. Such artificial adornments are little befitting to the wives of honest burghers."

"But rely upon it," replied the master-cutler, "that as soon as it is known that you have no hair, the girls of the city, envious of your beauty, will give you the nickname of *Mariquita the Bald*!"

"They may do so," replied Maria, "and that they may see that I do not care a fig for this or any other nickname, I swear to you that from this day forth I will not suffer anybody to call me by another name than *Mariquita the Bald*."

This was the event that rendered so famous throughout all Castile the beautiful daughter of good Juan Lanas, who in effect married Master Palomo, and became one of the most honorable and prolific women of the most illustrious city of Toledo.

THE LOVE OF CLOTILDE

Armando Palacio Valdés

In the dressing-room of Clotilde, leading actress of one of the most important theaters in the capital, there gathered every night about half a dozen of her male friends. The reception lasted almost always about as long as the performances; but it included a number of parentheses. Whenever the actress, was obliged to change her costume she would turn towards her visitors with a bewitching smile and beseeching eyes:

"Gentlemen, will you withdraw for one little moment?—not more than one little moment."

Thereupon they would all transfer themselves to the ante-room and remain there patiently waiting. No, I am mistaken, not quite all, because the youngest of them, a third year student in the School of Medicine, would avail himself of the chance to take a turn in the wings to stretch his legs and snatch a fugitive kiss or so. At all events, the majority remained, either seated or pacing up and down, until the moment when Clotilde would re-open her door and, putting out her head, decked as queen or peasant girl, according to the part she was playing, would call out:

"Now you may come back, gentlemen. Have I been very long?"

Don Jerónimo always lingered. He was the last to withdraw grumbling and the first to return to the dressing-room. He was never able to reconcile himself to that modest custom. And although he never allowed himself to say so openly, yet in the depths of his secret thoughts he regarded it as a lack of courtesy that he should be ejected from his seat, merely because the silly child must change her dress,—he, who for thirty years had passed his life behind the scenes and had been on intimate terms with every actor and actress, ancient and modern!

He was fifty-four years of age and had been attached to the Ministry of Foreign Affairs ever since he was four-and-twenty. Each successive government had regarded him as one of the indispensable wheels in the machinery of colonial administration. Furthermore, he was a bachelor and living at the mercy of his landlady. It was said that in his youth he once wrote a play which won him nothing but hisses and free entry for life behind the scenes of the theaters. Whether resigned or not to the verdict of the public, he ceased to write plays and assumed instead the nobler rôle of patron to unrecognized authors and artists and to ruined managers.

Any youth from the provinces who arrived in Madrid with a drama in his pocket could take no surer road to seeing it produced than that which led to the home of Don Jerónimo. One and all, he received them with open arms, the good and the bad alike. There is no denying that, since he was rather brusque in his ways, he never spared the young authors who asked his advice and read him their productions, but criticized vigorously, even to the verge of insult: "This whole episode is sheer nonsense; spill your ink-well on it!" "Why, look here, for the love of heaven! How do you suppose that a man who is on the point of committing murder is going to stand there for sixteen seconds, without drawing his breath?" "Lord, what tommyrot! Platonic love for a woman of that class! You must have tumbled out of the nest unfledged, my lad!"

But anyone possessed of a little tact refused to take offense, but went calmly on and ended by intrusting his manuscript to the hands of Don Jerónimo. And he could rest assured that his drama would be produced. The veteran of the greenrooms exercised a strong influence, akin to intimidation, over managers and actors alike; when he was displeased, he gave his tongue free rein; if a play had been hissed, he would protest, boiling with rage, against the public verdict, and would continue to support the author more stanchly than ever. If on the contrary it scored a hit, he merely kept silent and smiled ecstatically, but never sought out the successful author in order to congratulate him. And if the latter should complain of his indifference, his answer was:

"Now that you have shown that you can use your wings, will you please, my friend, will you please leave me free to succor some other poor fellow?"

His private life offered little of special interest. Every night, upon leaving the theater, he betook himself to the *Café Habanero,* where he habitually consumed a beefsteak, together with a small measure of beer. And, according to a certain friend, who had watched him repeatedly, he always managed his repast so artfully as to finish, at one and the same time, the last mouthful of meat, the last fragment of bread, and the last draught of beer.

On this particular night the little gathering was unwontedly animated. The actress's friends indulged more freely than usual in gossip and laughter. Don Jerónimo, muffled closely in his cape (one of his privileges), lounging at ease in the big corner chair, and with his inevitable cigar between his teeth (another special privilege), was giving utterance to rare and racy stories, which from time to time caused his hearers to cast a glance in the direction of Clotilde and brought a slightly heightened color to the latter's cheeks.

Don Jerónimo himself took no notice of this; he had first known her as such a mere child that he considered he had the right to dispense with certain courtesies that are due to ladies,—assuming that in the whole course of his life he had ever shown them to any woman, which is very doubtful. He had met her first as a mere child and had opened the way for her to the stage. At the time that he ran across her, she was living wretchedly and trying to learn the art of making artificial flowers. Today, thanks to her talent, she earned enough to keep her mother and sisters in comfort.

Clotilde's attraction lay in her charm of manner rather than her beauty. Her complexion was olive, her eyes large and black, the best of all her features; her mouth somewhat big, but with bright red lips and admirably even teeth. Tonight she was costumed as a lady of the time of Louis XV, with powdered hair, which was marvelously becoming to her. She took almost no part in the conversation, but seemed satisfied to be merely a listener, constantly turning her serene gaze from one speaker to another, and often answering only with a smile when they addressed her.

All at once there came the voice of the call-boy:

"Señorita Clotilde, if you please—"

"Coming," she answered, rising.

She crossed over to the mirror, gave a few final touches to her brows and lashes with a pencil, adjusted with somewhat nervous fingers the coils of her hair, the cross of brilliants which she wore at her throat, and the folds of her dress. Her friends became for the moment silent and abstractedly watched these last preparations.

"Good-by for the present, gentlemen." And she left the dressing-room, followed by her maid, carefully bearing her train, a magnificent train of cream-colored satin.

"She grows lovelier every day, Clotilde does," said the medical student, allowing an imperceptible sigh to escape him.

Don Jerónimo took an enormous pull at his cigar, and instantly became enveloped in a cloud of smoke. For this reason no one observed the smile of triumph with which he received the medical student's remark.

"I agree with you that she grows prettier every day," said another of the visitors. "But it seems to me that her disposition has been undergoing a big change for some time back. You, my boy, have not known her as long as we have. She used to be a fascinating talker, so merry, so full of spirits! No one could ever remain out of temper in her company. But now I find her grave and sad almost all the time."

"It's a fact that I have wondered at the melancholy look in her eyes."

Don Jerónimo took another enormous pull at his cigar. No one saw the swift flare of anger that passed over his face.

"Changes like that, my boy, have only one cause, and that is love."

"Was she engaged?"

"Precisely,—Don Jerónimo knows the story well."

"Yes, and I am going to tell it to you," said the one referred to, from the depths of his cloak. "Though you may believe me that it is no pleasant task to relate such follies. But it concerns a girl whom we all of us love, and whatever affects her ought to interest us.

"Some three years ago a young man, faultlessly dressed and with the manuscript of a play under his arm, called upon the director of this theater. Now there is nothing in the world more impressive and awe-inspiring than a well-dressed young man who carries the manuscript of a play under his arm. The director did his best to dodge him, and held him off with a number of adroit moves; but he was finally cornered, all the same. In other words, the young man invited him to breakfast one day, enticing him with the seductive prospect of several dozen oysters, washed down with abundant Sauterne, and for dessert he shot off his play at close range.

"As it turned out, the play was no good. Pepe did what you know one does in such cases: he expressed deep admiration for the versification, he said 'bravo!' over certain obscurely phrased thoughts, and finally he recommended a few changes in the second act, after which the work would be unexceptionable.

"The unwary poet returned home greatly pleased, and set to work zealously upon the revision. At the end of a fortnight he returned for another interview with Pepe; this time the latter found the first act somewhat slow, and advised him at any cost to put more action into it and make it somewhat shorter. It took the poet a month to rewrite the first act. When he once more presented himself, the director, while expressing great admiration for the excellence of the verse and for some of the ideas, manifested some doubt as to whether the play was *actable*. That it was *literary*, he had none whatever; on the contrary, it seemed to him that from this point of view it compared favorably with the best of Ayala's plays,—but actable, really actable, ah! that was another matter!"

"What is the difference, Don Jerónimo? I don't understand."

"Then I will explain, my boy. We, who are behind the scenes, mean by *actable* a good play, and by *literary* a bad one."

"I see!"

"After expressing these doubts, the manager concluded by recommending certain additional alterations in the third act.

"At last the poet understood,—a really marvelous occurrence, because poets, who understand everything else and can tell you why the condor flies so high, who soar to the skies and descend into the abyss and penetrate the secret thoughts of all created things, are not capable of realizing that there are times when their works do not please those who hear them. Our young man, whom we will call Inocencio, received back his manuscript somewhat peevishly, and for a while nothing further was heard of him. But at last, doubtless after a good deal of profound meditation, he presented himself on a certain morning at the home of Clotilde. I hardly need tell you that he carried his manuscript under his arm.

"He waited patiently in the parlor while our young friend completed her toilet, and when at last she made her appearance, she saw before her a blushing and confused young man, who nevertheless was pleasant-mannered and fashionably dressed, and who besought with stammering lips that she would do him the favor of listening while he read his play. Women, you must know, find a singular pleasure in playing the rôle of patroness, especially in regard to young men of pleasant manners and fashionable dress. So that it is not at all surprising that Clotilde listened patiently to the play and even pronounced it acceptable.

"The young man intrusted himself wholly to her guidance, deposited his manuscript in her pretty hands, as though it were a new-born child, and she received it like a doting mother, took it under her protection, and promised to watch over its precious existence and introduce it to the world. The young man declared that such an intention was worthy of the noble heart whose fame had already reached his ears. Clotilde replied that it was no kindness on her part to work to have the play produced, but only an act of justice. The young man said that this idea was exceedingly flattering, because Clotilde's great talent and the accuracy of her judgments were well known to everyone, but that he dared not build upon such an illusion. Clotilde declared that there were many unmerited reputations in the world, and one of them was hers, but that on this occasion she felt that she was on firm ground.

"The young man replied that when the river roars the water toils, and that when the whole world unites in admiring not only the exceptional beauty and artistic inspiration of a certain person, but also her splendid genius and brilliant intellect, it was necessary to bow one's head. Clotilde said that on this occasion she refused to bow hers, because she was quite convinced that the world was greatly mistaken regarding what it called her talent, which was nothing more nor less than pure instinct. The young man cried out to heaven against such mystification, for which there was absolutely no excuse. Then, promptly calming down, he declared himself profoundly moved by the modesty of his patroness, and swore by all the saints in heaven that he never had met her equal,—with the result that the manuscript was momentarily gaining ground in the heart of our sympathetic friend, and that the young man, overwhelmed with emotion, took his leave of her until the following day.

"On the following day, Clotilde called upon the manager, and by threatening to break her contract, forced from him a promise to produce Inocencio's play as soon as possible. That same afternoon, the poet expressed his thanks to his patroness and promptly took her into his confidence. He belonged to a distinguished provincial family, although without great financial resources. It was in the hope of bettering them that he had come to Madrid, relying solely upon his genius. In his native town they said that he had talent, and that if the verses which he had contributed to the *Tagus Echo* had been published in Madrid, he would be talked of as a second Nuñez de Arce y Grilo. He did not know whether that was so; but he felt that his heart was full of noble sentiments, and he loved the theater better than the apple of his eye. Would he succeed in being an Ayala or a Tamayo? Would he be rejected by the public? It was an insoluble mystery to him.

"During this interview, Clotilde became convinced of two very important things: namely, that Inocencio possessed a talent so great that his head could scarcely hold it, and secondly, that there was no one else in all Madrid who could wear so conspicuous a necktie with such charming effect. I need not tell you that their confidential interviews increased in frequency, and that consequently Clotilde came day by day more completely under the fascinating influence of that supernatural necktie. In the end, she yielded herself vanquished, and surrendered herself to it, bound hand and foot. The necktie deigned to raise her from the ground and grant her the favor of its affection."

"What about a necktie?" asked one of the company, who had been nodding.

Don Jerónimo took an immense, an infernal pull at his cigar, in testimony of his annoyance, then proceeded with no further notice:

"Meanwhile the rehearsals of Inocencio's play had begun. It was called, if I am not mistaken, *Stooping to Conquer*,—excuse me, no, I believe it was just the reverse, *Conquering to Stoop*. Well, at all events, it contained a participle and an infinitive. Before long I became aware that lover-like relations had been established between our fair friend and the author, and since, as a matter of fact, even if Inocencio was a bad poet, as Pepe insisted, he seemed like a good lad, I was very glad it had happened and I helped it along as much as I could. Clotilde confided in me, and declared that she was desperately in love; that her ambitions no longer had anything to do with the art of the stage, which seemed to her an unbearable slavery; that her ideal was to live tranquilly, even if it were in a garret, united to the man whom she adored; that woman was born to be the guardian angel of the fireside, and not to divert the public, and that she herself would rather be queen of a humble little apartment illuminated with love, than to receive all the applause in the world. In short, gentlemen, our young friend was living in the midst of an idyllic dream.

"Inocencio was, to all appearance, no less in love than she. I frequently encountered them walking through the unfrequented by-paths of the Retiro, at a respectable distance from her mother, who lingered opportunely to examine the first opening buds of flowers or some curious insect. Mothers, at this critical period of courtship, are under an obligation to be admirers of the works of nature. The young pair of turtle-doves would pause when they caught sight of me and greet me blushingly. I cannot conceal from you that, however much I felt the loss to art, I was delighted that Clotilde was going to be married. A woman always needs the protection of a man. And there is no question that so far as outward appearance went, they were worthy of one another. Inocencio certainly was a most attractive young fellow.

"At the theater they talked of nothing else than of this wedding, which was still in the bud. Everybody was delighted, because Clotilde is the only actress, since the beginning of the world, who took it into her head to attempt what until now was regarded as impossible, to make herself beloved by her companions.

"I observed, nevertheless,—for you know that I am an observant person: it is the only quality that I possess, that of observation, a thing to which the authors of today attach no importance. Today, in the drama, everything is so much dried leaves, a lot of moonshine, which, they let filter down through the foliage of the trees, a lot of description of dawn and twilight, and a lot of other similar pastry-shop stuff. That's all there is to it! When any fledgling author comes to me with nonsense of that sort, I say to him: 'Get down to the facts! Get down to the facts!' The facts are the drama, which doesn't exist in the great part of the above-mentioned."

"Aren't you exciting yourself, Don Jerónimo?"

"Well, as I was telling you, I observed that as the rehearsals progressed the ascendency of Inocencio over our young friend increased. The tone in which he addressed her was no longer the humble and courteous tone of earlier days; he corrected her frequently in her manner of delivery, he dictated the attitudes and gestures which she should adopt, and sometimes, when the actress did not quite understand his wishes, he allowed himself to address her publicly in rather severe terms, and the way he looked at her was severer still. Our poet was already thundering and lightning like a true lord and master.

"Clotilde accepted it with good grace. She, who had always been so haughty, even towards the most distinguished authors, stretched out and shrank back like soft wax in the hands of that insignificant jackanapes. You ought to have seen the humility with which she accepted his suggestions, and the distress which his censures caused her. All the time that the rehearsal lasted she kept her eyes steadily fixed upon him, watching like a submissive slave to catch the wishes of her master. The poet, lolling at ease in an arm-chair, with a brazier of hot coals before him, directed the action in as dictatorial a manner as either Gracia Gutierrez or Ayala could have done. A mere glance from him sufficed to make Clotilde flush crimson or turn pale. The other actors made no protest, out of consideration for her. When she had finished her scene she came eagerly to take her seat beside her betrothed, who sometimes deigned to welcome her with a haughty smile, and at other times with an Olympian indifference. I, meanwhile, looked on, scandalized.

"On one occasion I came upon them from behind, and overheard what they were saying. Clotilde was speaking, and hotly maintaining that Inocencio's *Stooping to Conquer* or *Conquering to Stoop* was better than *A New Drama*. The young man protested feebly. On another occasion they were speaking of their future union. Clotilde was picturing in impassioned phrases the nook to which they would go to hide their happiness; some lofty spot on the hills of Salamanca, a dear little nest, bathed in sunlight, where Inocencio could work in his private study, writing plays, while she sat by his side and embroidered in absolute silence. When he was tired they could talk for a while, to let him rest, and then she would give him a kiss and go back again to her work. In the evening they would go out, arm in arm, to take a short walk, and then home again. But no more of the theater; she abhorred it

with all her soul. In the spring they would go every morning to take a walk in the Retiro and take chocolate under the trees; in the summer they would spend a month or two in Inocencio's birthplace, so as to bring back from the country a supply of good color and health for the coming winter.

"The description of this tender idyl, which, even if I am a confirmed bachelor, set my heart beating within my breast, produced no other effect upon the new author than an insolent somnolence which would not disappear until he suddenly raised his imperious voice to admonish some one of the actors.

"At last the opening night arrived. We were all anxious to see the result. The prevailing opinion was that the play offered little novelty; but since Clotilde had staked her whole soul upon the outcome, a big success was predicted. At the dress rehearsal our young friend had achieved genuine prodigies. There was a moment when the few of us whom curiosity had brought to witness it, rose to our feet electrified, convulsed, making a most unseemly outcry. You have no conception how marvelously she rendered her part. Then and there, all of a sudden, an idea entered my head. Recalling all my observations of Clotilde's love affair, I felt convinced, in view of the evidence, that Inocencio had had no other purpose in winning her love than to assure an exceptional interpretation of the leading *rôle* of his play, and a flattering outcome of his venture. I decided not to communicate my suspicions to anyone. I kept silent and hoped, but there is no doubt that from that time on the young man was decidedly out of favor with me.

"The noise which Inocencio's friends had been making in regard to the theme of his play, the fact that Clotilde had chosen it for her benefit performance, and the wide-spread rumor that the celebrated actress was going to win a signal triumph in it, all worked together to help the speculators to dispose of every seat in the house at fabulous prices. I know a marquis who paid eleven *duros* for two orchestra stalls. This room where we are now sitting was filled, just as it is annually, with flowers and presents; it was impossible to move about in the midst of such a conglomeration of porcelain, books with costly bindings, ebony work-boxes, picture-frames, and no end of other fancy trifles.

"The audience room was unusually brilliant. The most resplendent ladies, the men most distinguished in politics, literature, and finance; in short, the *high life*, as the phrase goes, was all there. But even more brilliant and more radiant was Inocencio himself; radiant with glory and happiness, and graciously receiving the crowds of visitors who came to see the presents, dictating orders to the call-boys and scene-shifters regarding the proper setting of the scene, and multiplying his smiles and hand-shakings to the

point of infinity. Clotilde also seemed more beautiful than ever, and her expressive face revealed the tender emotion which possessed her, as well as her deep anxiety to win laurels for her future husband.

"The curtain arose and everyone hurried to occupy his seat. In the wings there was no one save the author and three or four of his friends. The opening scenes were received as usual with indifference; the following ones with a little more cordiality; the versification was fluent and polished, and, as you know, the public appreciates sugar-coated phrases. At last the moment arrived for Clotilde's entrance, and a faint murmur of curiosity and expectation ran through the audience. She spoke her lines discreetly, but without much warmth; it was easy to see that she was afraid. The curtain fell in a dead silence.

"Immediately the waiting-room and passage-way were filled by Inocencio's friends, who came eagerly to tell him that this first performance of his play was a great success,—but what was the matter with Clotilde? She hardly put any movement into her part,—and she was usually so much alive, so tremendously forceful! Our young friend acknowledged that, as a matter of fact, she had felt badly scared, and that this had hampered her seriously. The author, greatly alarmed for the fate of his work, endeavored to persuade her that there was nothing to be afraid of, that all she had to do was to be herself, and that she was not to think of him at all while she spoke her lines.

"'I can't help it,' insisted Clotilde, 'all the time that I am speaking I keep thinking that you are the author, and imagining that the play is not going to succeed, and it makes me so frightened.'

"Inocencio was in despair; he tried entreaties, advice, arguments, he embraced her without caring who saw him; he tried to infuse courage into her by appealing to her vanity as an artist; in short, he did everything imaginable to save his play.

"The second act began. Clotilde had a few pathetic scenes. In the beginning there was a certain slight disturbance in the audience, and this sufficed to disconcert her completely, and to make her acting irremediably bad, worse than she had ever acted in her whole life. A good deal of coughing was heard, and some loud murmurs of impatience. At the end of that second act a few indiscreet friends tried to applaud, but the audience drowned them out with an immense and terrifying series of hisses. The author, who was standing by my side, pale as death, relieved his feelings with a flood of coarse words, and made his way to Pepe's room, which faces that of Clotilde, and where his friends consoled him, casting the whole blame for the failure upon her, and inflaming more and more the anger surging in

his heart. Meanwhile, our friend was utterly crushed and overcome, and continually calling for her Inocencio. In order to spare her further trouble, I told her that the author had accepted the situation resignedly, and had left the theater to get a breath of air. The unhappy girl bitterly blamed herself, taking the entire failure on her own shoulders.

"The curtain rose for the third act; and we all gathered anxiously at the wings. Clotilde, by a powerful effort of will, showed herself at first more self-possessed than in the previous acts, but the audience was in a mood to have some sport, and nothing could have made them take the play seriously. When the public once scents a trail, it is like a wild beast that smells blood; there is no way of heading it off, and you have got to let it have its flesh at any cost. And there is no doubt that on this occasion it gorged itself full. Coughs, laughter, sneezes, stampings, hisses,—there was a little of everything. Tears sprang to our poor friend's eyes, and she seemed upon the point of fainting. When the curtain finally fell her eyes sought on all sides for her lover, but he had disappeared. In her dressing-room, where I followed her, she sobbed, groaned, gave way to despair, called herself a fool, said that she was going to hire herself out on some farm to tend the geese and more to the same effect. It cost me some hard work to calm her down, but at last I succeeded so that she sank into a sort of silent lethargy. In the sorrow which her eyes revealed I saw that what tormented her horribly was the absence of Inocencio.

"The door of the room was suddenly flung open. The defeated poet made his appearance; he was quite pale but apparently calm. Nevertheless, I perceived at the first glance that his calmness was assumed, and that the smile which contracted his lips closely resembled that of a condemned man who wishes to die bravely.

"A gleam of joy illuminated Clotilde's face. She rose swiftly and flung her arms around his neck, saying in a broken voice:

"'I have ruined you, my poor Inocencio, I have ruined you! How generous you are! But listen, I swear to you, by the memory of my father, that I will atone for the humiliation you have just suffered.'

"'There is no need for you to atone, my dear girl,' replied the poet, in a soft tone under which a disdainful anger could be felt, 'my family has not achieved its illustrious name through the intercession of any actor. From this day henceforth I gladly renounce the theater and all that is connected with it. Accordingly,—I wish you good-day.' And, unclasping the arms that imprisoned his neck, and smiling sarcastically, he retreated a few steps and took his leave. Clotilde gazed at him in a stupor, then fell unconscious on the divan.

"At the sight of her in such a state I felt my blood take fire, and I followed the young man out. I overtook him near the stairs, and, grasping him by the wrist, I said to him:

"'A word with you. The first thing that a man has to be, before he can be a poet, is a gentleman,—and that is something you are not. Your play was hissed because it lacks the same thing that you lack,—and that is a heart. Here, sir, is my card.'"

"And did you not send him your seconds, Don Jerónimo?" inquired the medical student.

"Silence, silence!" exclaimed another of the group, "here is Clotilde."

And, in fact, the charming actress at that moment appeared in the doorway, and her large and sad black eyes, all the more beautiful beneath her white Louis XV coiffure, smiled tenderly upon her faithful friends.

CAPTAIN VENENO'S PROPOSAL OF MARRIAGE

Pedro Antonio de Alarcón

"Great heavens! What a woman!" cried the captain, and stamped with fury. "Not without reason have I been trembling and in fear of her from the first time I saw her! It must have been a warning of fate that I stopped playing *écarté* with her. It was also a bad omen that I passed so many sleepless nights. Was there ever mortal in a worse perplexity than I am? How can I leave her alone without a protector, loving her, as I do, more than my own life? And, on the other hand, how can I marry her, after all my declaimings against marriage?"

Then turning to Augustias—"What would they say of me in the club? What would people say of me, if they met me in the street with a woman on my arm, or if they found me at home, just about to feed a child in swaddling clothes? I—to have children? To worry about them? To live in eternal fear that they might fall sick or die? Augustias, believe me, as true as there is a God above us, I am absolutely unfit for it! I should behave in such a way that after a short while you would call upon heaven either to be divorced or to become a widow. Listen to my advice: do not marry me, even if I ask you."

"What a strange creature you are," said the young woman, without allowing herself to be at all discomposed, and sitting very erect in her chair. "All that you are only telling to yourself! From what do you conclude that I wish to be married to you; that I would accept your offer, and that I should not prefer living by myself, even if I had to work day and night, as so many girls do who are orphans?"

"How do I come to that conclusion?" answered the captain with the greatest candor. "Because it cannot be otherwise. Because we love each other. Because we are drawn to each other. Because a man such as I, and a woman such as you, cannot live in any other way! Do you suppose I do not understand that? Don't you suppose I have reflected on it before now? Do you think I am indifferent in your good name and reputation? I have spoken plainly in order to speak, in order to fly from my own conviction, in order to examine whether I can escape from this terrible dilemma which is robbing me of my sleep, and whether I can possibly find an expedient so that I need not marry you—to do which I shall finally be compelled, if you stand by your resolve to make your way alone!"

"Alone! Alone!" repeated Augustias, roguishly. "And why not with a worthier companion? Who tells you that I shall not some day meet a man whom I like, and who is not afraid to marry me?"

"Augustias! let us skip that!" growled the captain, his face turning scarlet.

"And why should we not talk about it?"

"Let us pass over that, and let me say, at the same time, that I will murder the man who dares to ask for your hand. But it is madness on my part to be angry without any reason. I am not so dull as not to see how we two stand. Shall I tell you? We love each other. Do not tell me I am mistaken! That would be lying. And here is the proof: if you did not love me, I, too, should not love you! Let us try to meet one another halfway. I ask for a delay of ten years. When I shall have completed my half century, and when, a feeble old man, I shall have become familiar with the idea of slavery, then we will marry without anyone knowing about it. We will leave Madrid, and go to the country, where we shall have no spectators, where there will be nobody to make fun of me. But until this happens, please take half of my income secretly, and without any human soul ever knowing anything about it. You continue to live here, and I remain in my house. We will see each other, but only in the presence of witnesses—for instance, in society. We will write to each other every day. So as not to endanger your good name, I will never pass through this street, and on Memorial Day only we will go to the cemetery together with Rosa."

Augustias could not but smile at the last proposal of the good captain, and her smile was not mocking, but contented and happy, as if some cherished hope had dawned in her heart, as if it were the first ray of the sun of happiness which was about to rise in her heaven! But being a woman—though as brave and free from artifices as few of them—she yet managed to subdue the signs of joy rising within her. She acted as if she cherished not the slightest hope, and said with a distant coolness which is usually the special and genuine sign of chaste reserve:

"You make yourself ridiculous with your peculiar conditions. You stipulate for the gift of an engagement-ring, for which nobody has yet asked you."

"I know still another way out—for a compromise, but that is really the last one. Do you fully understand, my young lady from Aragon? It is the last way out, which a man, also from Aragon, begs leave to explain to you."

She turned her head and looked straight into his eyes, with an expression indescribably earnest, captivating, quiet, and full of expectation.

The captain had never seen her features so beautiful and expressive; at that moment she looked to him like a queen.

"Augustias," said, or rather stammered, this brave soldier, who had been under fire a hundred times, and who had made such a deep impression on the young girl through his charging under a rain of bullets like a lion, "I have the honor to ask for your hand on one certain, essential, unchangeable condition. Tomorrow morning—today—a soon as the papers are in order—as quickly as possible. I can live without you no longer!"

The glances of the young girl became milder, and she rewarded him for his decided heroism with a tender and bewitching smile.

"But I repeat that it is on one condition," the bold warrior hastened to repeat, feeling that Augustias's glances made him confused and weak.

"On what condition?" asked the young girl, turning fully round, and now holding him under the witchery of her sparkling black eyes.

"On the condition," he stammered, "that, in case we have children, we send them to the orphanage. I mean—on this point I will never yield. Well, do you consent? For heaven's sake, say yes!"

"Why should I not consent to it, Captain Veneno?" answered Augustias, with a peal of laughter. "You shall take them there yourself, or, better still, we both of us will take them there. And we will give them up without kissing them, or anything else! Don't you think we shall take them there?"

Thus spoke Augustias, and looked at the captain with exquisite joy in her eyes. The good captain thought he would die of happiness; a flood of tears burst from his eyes; he folded the blushing girl in his arms, and said:

"So I am lost?"

"Irretrievably lost, Captain Veneno," answered Augustias.

One morning in May, 1852—that is, four years after the scene just described—a friend of mine, who told me this story, stopped his horse in front of a mansion on San Francisco Avenue, in Madrid; he threw the reins to his groom, and asked the long-coated footman who met him at the door:

"Is your master at home?"

"If your honor will be good enough to walk upstairs, you will find him in the library. His excellency does not like to have visitors announced. Everybody can go up to him directly."

"Fortunately I know the house thoroughly," said the stranger to himself, while he mounted the stairs. "In the library! Well, well, who would have thought of Captain Veneno ever taking to the sciences?"

Wandering through the rooms, the visitor met another servant, who repeated, "The master is in the library." And at last he came to the door of the room in question, opened it quickly, and stood, almost turned to stone for astonishment, before the remarkable group which it offered to his view.

In the middle of the room, on the carpet which covered the floor, a man was crawling on all-fours. On his back rode a little fellow about three years old, who was kicking the man's sides with his heels. Another small boy, who might have been a year and a half old, stood in front of the man's head, and had evidently been tumbling his hair. One hand held the father's neckerchief, and the little fellow was tugging at it as if it had been a halter, shouting with delight in his merry child's voice:

"Gee up, donkey! Gee up!"